www.somethingwickedlyweird.com

To read more about Stanley, look out for all the
Something Wickedly Weird books:

The Werewolf and the Ibis
The Ice Pirates
The Buccaneer's Bones
The Curse of the Wolf
The Smugglers' Secret
The Golden Labyrinth

Read more spooky tales in Dust 'n' Bones,
also by the award-winning Chris Mould.

And visit Chris at his website:
www.chrismouldink.com

THE CURSE OF THE WOLF

CHRIS MOULD

Hodder Children's Books

A division of Hachette Children's Books

For Sue, Emily and Charlotte

Text and illustrations copyright © 2008 Chris Mould

First published in Great Britain in 2008
by Hodder Children's Books
This paperback edition published 2010

The right of Chris Mould to be identified as the Author and Illustrator
of the Work has been asserted by him in accordance with the
Copyright, Designs and Patents Act 1988.

1

A Catalogue record for this book is available from the British Library

ISBN 978 0 340 98919 7

Printed and bound in the UK by
CPI Bookmarque Ltd, Croydon, CR0 4TD

The paper and board used in this paperback by Hodder Children's Books
are natural recyclable products made from wood grown in sustainable
forests. The manufacturing processes conform to the environmental
regulations of the country of origin.

Hodder Children's Books
A division of Hachette Children's Books
338 Euston Road, London NW1 3BH
An Hachette UK company
www.hachette.co.uk

Admiral Buggles

Crampton Rock

The Warning

Stanley Buggles was standing in the drawing room of Candlestick Hall, looking over the portrait of his great-uncle, Admiral Swift. He wished he could tell him all that had happened since he'd inherited the old place from him. That he had finally got his hands on the ancient silver casket, and that it contained the six candles the Admiral himself had searched for.

And that right now a pan was warming them
in the kitchen, melting them down to retrieve
what lay hidden inside.

Outside the Hall, the wind had picked up.
The grass blew in circles around the lawn,
the sun shone through the windows and the
breeze sent the flower tops dancing here
and there.

Crack, crack, came an unfamiliar noise that
drew Stanley to the window. A carrion crow
was standing on the ledge,
pecking at the glass.

Stanley went right up to it but it wasn't afraid. It was going berserk, flapping and beating its dark cloak and staring right at him. *Crack, crack,* it continued.

'Shoo, shoo,' said Stanley. 'Go on!' He banged back at it on the pane until it took off. This was not like Stanley – he was a great bird lover, and normally he would have stared at it all day, being so close, but it had spooked him.

'Do you have a minute, lad?' came Victor's voice, distracting him from his thoughts.

Victor had settled in well since his return to the island a few weeks before. Both he and Mrs Carelli, his wife, made good house-keepers. He did the gardens and repair work. She did the cooking and cleaning. Stanley did … well, not much, but then again the place did belong to him. He wasn't lazy, he was just busy doing nothing, he would joke – and then he would be off on some adventure through the house.

Things had changed for Stanley recently: he was going to make a permanent home on Crampton Rock. He had decided, along with his mother, that he would live there under the supervision of Mr and Mrs Carelli. And yes, his mother would visit from time to time, but mostly he would be out here on the Rock alone – and so far, he was loving every minute.

'How about that, lad? Is that how you wanted it?' asked Victor. He was pointing to the pike on the wall. He was in a spanking new, freshly polished glass case – just like his old one, but better. And he was back in his favourite spot under the back of the staircase.

'Excellent,' said Stanley. 'Thank you, Victor. He will be delighted, I'm sure.'

And as they walked away the pike was

already mumbling away to himself.

'About time too,' he grumbled. 'I couldn't have stayed in that old cupboard a moment longer. I have had quite enough by way of wild adventures and being hurled around from one place to another. I should be quite happy to remain here for now, thank you very much.'

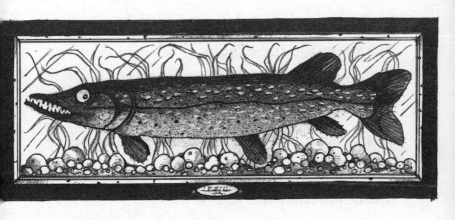

Finally, the pike settled into a long sleep. But as he slept, something disturbed him.

He dreamed that a black cloud settled over the house, and that darkness was about to descend in some strange form.

Victor had turned to outside duties and Stanley was alone in the kitchen. He stood over the stove and waited impatiently for the wax to turn to a clear liquid. And as it did, six pieces of parchment became clear. Each was curled up from its long sleep, hidden inside the candles.

Stanley picked them out of the pan and turned them out on to the table. When all of them had cooled down, he fiddled around with the paper, flattening the pieces and fitting together the jigsaw.

Once he had put the pieces together, he could see that they held a complex set of instructions. But there was a large hole in the middle of the puzzle! It was almost as if a diagram had been scissored out of the centre, with scribbled indications around it pointing this way and that. Why was the map not complete? It made no sense.

Just as Stanley was mulling over this dilemma, Victor returned.

'I'm sorry to bother you again, lad, but you must come outside and take a look at this.'

'At what?' asked Stanley. But Victor was already out of the door.

Stanley gathered the pieces of his map and bundled them carefully into a drawer on his way through the hallway. He would place them in his room shortly. The door was open and Stanley walked outside to find Victor standing on the long pathway and staring upwards.

What looked like a thousand crows had descended on to the roof of Candlestick Hall,

squawking and flapping and making a terrible
din. There were so many they seemed to
darken the sky.

Stanley had often seen the birds
resting on a building in the village,

but for now they
had claimed
the lid of his
house as
their own.

What had brought
them here?

Victor and Stanley were joined by Mrs
Carelli, returning from the village. She was
armed with bags of this and that, and stood
craning her neck up at the black veil that
covered the tiles.

'What on earth is that all about?' she
called.

'Perhaps it *means* something,' said Stanley.

He knew enough about carrion crows not to trust them. Dressed like funeral guests in their dark hoods and sooty black coats, they were the craftiest of egg thieves and would think nothing of preying on young chicks.

Before Stanley and Victor could turn inside, one of the crows abruptly swooped down and took a fierce peck at Stanley. It clawed at him and its feet got stuck in his long hair.

Mrs Carelli batted it off. 'Shoo, shoo!' Victor swung his rake in the air as the bird persisted in attacking Stanley. The three of them fumbled towards the doorway, but the bird hung on still. In panic, Stanley closed his hands around its body and hurled it back into the air as they ran inside.

Safe indoors, dishevelled and shaken, they turned to each other and laughed. Pulling themselves back together, they looked out through the window that took in the view of the harbour. Some crows had landed on the front lawn and one was at the window again, pecking.

Stanley's face grew serious. He watched for a while, until the birds returned to the roof.

'I've never seen no such birds attacking anyone, Victor,' Mrs Carelli insisted, looking at him for an explanation.

Victor shrugged his shoulders. 'Must be something in the breeze.'

But Stanley had a feeling it was more than the weather that had changed the mood of these sinister creatures. He gathered the pieces of map and went upstairs where he pored over the details again, distracting himself from his thoughts of the baleful black birds.

The Darklings

Out on the moor, the gypsies were busying themselves with daily life. The children played in noisy bunches and the men were out gathering firewood or mending wagon wheels.

Greta was the wise old woman of the camp, the one they all turned to for help and advice. Right now, she was sitting at the table gazing uneasily into her glass ball. Smoke had clouded the vision in the glass, but now it cleared. A face, no, two faces. A man, and then a woman who walked behind him. But they were not alone. Three children trailed behind the woman in a straight line. They were parading through the village, then heading past the harbour, turning up towards Candlestick Hall.

And then the vision clouded over and it was lost.

'Aah, curses,' said Greta. 'Some foul deed tries to show itself in the glass, but the mist is thick and I cannot see. What is it this time? Someone seeks to darken Stanley's door, and for no good reason.' She sighed in frustration, covered the glass ball with its velvet cloth, and walked outside to take in the fresh air.

Back at the Hall, Stanley was showing the map to his close ally, Daisy Grouse. 'Look, Daisy. The map's quite clear, but there's a great gaping hole in the middle.'

There was no fooling Daisy; she had a good head on her shoulders. The pair of them made a good team and they were as thick as thieves. When Daisy wasn't at her uncle's home in the lighthouse, you could be sure she was here at the Hall.

'Let me try,' she insisted. She attempted to put the pieces together differently but no, Stanley was right. It looked like someone had torn a neat shape from its middle.

'What about our good friend the pike?' suggested Daisy. 'Does he know we have the map? Surely he can tell us something.'

'Maybe,' said Stanley. 'He's been busy settling into his new home, but he should be back to normal by now I would think.' They gathered up the pieces and ran downstairs.

Stanley knew only too well that the pike would speak if he felt the need to, but that he was not always in a talkative mood.

'We thought perhaps you might have an opinion on our map here!' said Stanley gingerly. 'There appears to be something missing from the middle. Does that mean anything to you?'

'I fear you have a far more pressing matter to attend to, my dear boy, and I would give it my fullest attention if you wish to remain at the Hall.'

Stanley stared at him in frustration, but that was all the pike would say.

BANG, BANG, BANG.

Someone was rapping heavily at the door. Daisy was quick to realize that the map's safety was always at risk, so she grabbed it and sneaked it into a nearby drawer.

Mrs Carelli was coming down the staircase and they all three met at the front door together.

'Ahhh ... erm ... Mister ... and Mrs ... Darkling, isn't it?' asked Mrs Carelli, opening the door. Stanley noticed that her voice seemed shaky.

Looking back at them was the strangest bunch of people Stanley and Daisy had ever seen.

'My name is Edmund Darkling, and this is my wife Grace,' explained the man standing in the doorway. He wore no expression, and his manner was cold and unnerving. 'This is our eldest daughter, Annabelle, and these are our twins, Olive and Berkeley.'

A long streak of a girl glared back at them and an identical-looking pair did the same. The younger girl carried a headless doll and her twin had his hands behind his back, with a look on his face that swore he was up to no good. They were dressed in deep, sombre colours with frilled sleeves and collars. All wore knitted brows and sullen mouths.

Stanley studied their faces. There was something shocking in their appearance, something unusual about their features, but he couldn't quite decide what it was. Their eyebrows were thick and black and maddened their eyes. Their hair was straight and thin.

Mr Darkling had paused before speaking again and Stanley felt as if he should say something, but it wouldn't come. He longed to shut the door on them, but his good manners betrayed him. He shifted nervously.

Right then, one of the crows descended from the roof, landed on Mr Darkling's hat and hopped down to rest peacefully on his shoulder.

'I have good reason to darken your door, Stanley,' he announced, staring directly at Stanley. 'Now listen carefully. I wish to inform you that, as the true and rightful owner of the Darkling residence, the one you now stand in and refer to as Candlestick Hall, I wish to return with my family so that we may resume our position here. There is much to do and we need you to vacate the premises within seven days.'

He said it almost as if what he said had no consequence for them. There was no emotion in his voice, no regret or embarrassment at the circumstances.

Stanley quickly made sense of what had just been said to him. The man now standing at his door was claiming to be the rightful owner of Candlestick Hall.

But Mrs Carelli's nervousness had already left her, her blood boiling at the thought that they could just walk to the door and absurdly lay claim to the house.

'Young Stanley Buggles here is the rightful owner of Candlestick Hall. He inherited it from his great-uncle, Admiral Swift. I am his housekeeper and I would thank you kindly, sir, if you would take your ridiculous claim and clear off our land,' she thundered.

She tried to shut the door, but the Darkling boy stepped quickly inside the frame and she stopped short of crushing his foot.

'Aah yes, Admiral Swift,' continued Mr

Darkling, his expression still unmoved. The
pirate who terrorized the Darklings and
forced us to give up the house when I was
a mere boy. It is hard to believe that the
pleasant-looking young man in front of me is
descended from a line of villainous piracy.
Now, will you please ensure that our things
are left behind when you leave? I would not
wish to find a ransacked house on my arrival.
We shall be here in a week. Unless of course,
you can prove your claim to this place.' He
lifted an evil smile from the corner of his
mouth.

The crow flew from his shoulder as all four
of them turned and left. As they marched
down the pathway, the twins turned at the
same time and stuck out their pointed
tongues at Stanley.

*

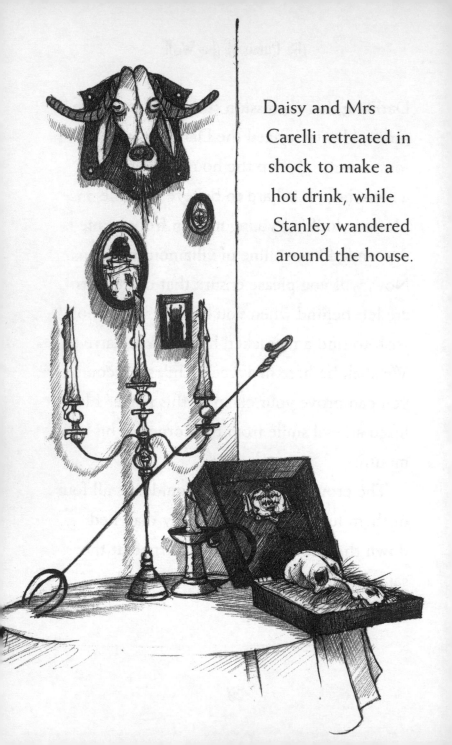

Daisy and Mrs Carelli retreated in shock to make a hot drink, while Stanley wandered around the house.

He took a good long look at all the weird
and wonderful things that filled the Hall from
top to bottom.

Animal heads in jars, skulls and skeletons,
stuffed wildlife caught in traps and snares.
He chewed over his thoughts of the unusual
family that had stood at his door.

Were all these things really *theirs*?

Were they really the rightful owners of
Candlestick Hall? And would he soon be
homeless on the island he had grown to love
so much?

3

The Loophole

'First things first. Forget the map for now,' said Daisy, as she returned it to Stanley's room and placed it back in the silver casket. She was the only one apart from Stanley who knew of the casket's home behind the false panel in the cupboard.

Next, they all sat around the kitchen table and got the papers out. Deeds, death

certificates, other documents that Stanley
knew would make sense to somebody, but
not to him.

'Victor, it was you yourself who recently
told me that the old place used to be named
Darkling Hall,' piped up Stanley.

'That's true, Stanley. But the Darklings
have lived in the village for many years
now. Your Great-Uncle Bart bought Darkling
Hall in good faith, I'm sure. We need to
go through all this with a fine-tooth comb,
lad.'

Victor looked over everything meticulously.
He read everything from back to front, inside
out and back again, peering over his glasses
and making little notes to himself on a long
sheet of paper.

Mrs Carelli was busying herself. 'I'll deal wi'
normality,' she said, as she cranked up the

wood burner in the kitchen and rolled out pastry, grumbling to herself about how the Darklings were 'a disgrace to common decency'.

Stanley and Daisy decided that they would take advice from the Mayoress of the Rock, so they headed into the village. But as soon as they left the Hall a crow appeared and danced around their feet, almost as if to stop them going anywhere. It didn't seem at all perturbed by their presence.

Two more birds appeared, their eyes glowing like little moons. Then abruptly there were five or six, clawing and pecking at Stanley's head. Daisy waved them off with her hands and they scratched at her with black talons.

They ran down to the village and could only escape by heading into the village hall, heaving the door closed behind them.

The Mayoress, Penelope Spoonbill, was standing there waiting, almost as if she had expected them. She was a slight woman, with her hair pulled back and a beak of a nose, and her hands clasped together. There was something fragile about her spindly form, but she had an air of authority about her.

'Good morning, Stanley. You seem a little flustered, but I see you have had the good sense to bring help and support. You may need it.'

'Why do you say that?' asked Stanley.

'I'm afraid our friend Mister Darkling is ahead of you, Stanley. He has already sought my advice, and he insists that Darkling Hall was taken from his family many years ago, when I myself was only a young girl. I recall nothing of his claim.'

'But why *now*?' asked Stanley.

'I think the Darklings feared your great-uncle, Stanley. And when you first came here you were beset with troubles of one kind and another. But you have solved many problems now for the Hall, and she sits in peace at last. You have done the work for them, and the time was right for them to make their move,' she argued.

'But his claim is ridiculous,' said Stanley, 'and no one would ever take it seriously. Surely the strict laws of Crampton Rock will protect us?'

'Of course, Stanley. No one has the right just to declare that something belongs to them, without foundation to their claim. It is up to them to prove their assertion, not you. I trust you have your deeds to hand?' the Mayoress asked.

'Yes, of course,' Stanley said, breathing a sigh of relief that he had found someone with good sense and authority who seemed to be in sympathy with his plight.

Penelope Spoonbill took out a large book entitled *Property Law.* 'Let's take a look and make it clear,' she said.

'You should be warned, though, that Mister Darkling has seen these details already. He must feel he has a hold over you.'

She opened the book at a marked page and ran a long finger down the paragraphs until she stopped and trailed back to the beginning of a long sentence. 'Here it is,' she said.

Where a dispute of ownership is contested, the presentation of property deeds shall establish the rightful owner unless proof to the contrary can be determined by evidence written in stone.

'What does that mean in plain speaking?' asked Daisy.

'Well, what it means,' began Miss Spoonbill, 'is that if Stanley has the deeds

and they show his name as being the owner
of the Candlestick estate, then he is fine.'

'And what about the last bit?' asked
Stanley. 'Something about "written in stone"?'

'Oh, don't worry about that, Stanley. It
means that if somewhere it was written in
stone that the Darklings owned the house
there would be an argument for their case.
We all know that's not really going to happen
now, is it. It's really an old way of saying,
"unless the impossible should happen", that's
all. These old documents are worded funnily
sometimes.'

But worry about it Stanley did. And before
he had even reached home again, his fears
had turned against him.

The light was dropping as they left the
village hall, and the Darkling twins were
hanging around outside the door. They stared

at Stanley as he and Daisy left the building, Olive nursing the headless doll in her arms.

'Hello, Stanley. Who's that?' Olive asked.

'Erm … hello, Olive,' replied Stanley. 'This is my friend Daisy.'

'Isn't she pretty!' she said and then both she and Berkeley ran away screaming and laughing into the darkness of the streets.

'I'm afraid they're … well, a little bit … odd,' muttered Stanley, almost feeling as if he had to apologize to Daisy on their behalf.

The fire baskets were burning in the harbour, and the lights in the windows lit the short trail back home.

But there was something going on outside the door of the Hall. A small group of people, three or four maybe, one of them holding a light. A faint clink, clink, clink resounded across the street.

Stanley noticed that the crows were still and silent on the roof. 'It must be the Darklings,' he insisted. 'Otherwise those birds would be going mad.'

Sure enough, Edmund Darkling was holding a lamplight up to the pillar at the right-hand side of the front door. Another man was chipping at the cement work with small masonry tools. Mr and Mrs Carelli were standing there too, looking most displeased.

'You have no right to be here,' complained Mrs Carelli. 'It's an outrage!'

'What's going on?' asked Stanley.

'Patience, please,' said Mr Darkling in his calm, deep tone. 'I do believe we are about to retrieve a result.'

But before Stanley could eke out an explanation, the situation had unravelled in front of his eyes.

The stonemason pulled at the now loose brickwork, and out came a large block. He turned it round and from its previously hidden side he rubbed away the years of dust and dirt to reveal a word, written in stone.

The Darkling Curse

'I'm sorry,' said Miss Spoonbill. 'I am not above the law. I see your problem, yet I feel there is nothing I can do.'

She was sitting in Candlestick Hall with Stanley and the Carellis, explaining the situation as it now stood. Now that 'proof in stone' had been revealed, the Darkling family had a claim on the house. This meant that it

was now possible that Candlestick Hall could
be put back in their hands.

'Until the case is settled in the court, the
Darkling family are allowed to reside in the
house. That is
the law of
the Rock.'

And no sooner had she left than the Darklings were arriving, leaving behind their home in the village. Between them, they pulled and pushed a long open-backed cart up the path, filled with odd things. A coffin stuffed with long coats, cloaks and tall hats. Macabre paintings of their grim-looking ancestors. Heaps of morbid-looking decorations. Strangely shaped jars and medicine bottles. Boxes of dusty handwritten books dribbled with candle wax. Long black velvet curtains.

Much of it, Stanley noticed, was like the things already in the house.

A stack of wooden boxes marked 'fragile' and 'do not touch' filled one end of the cart, strange hisses and rattles coming from them.

'What on earth have you got in there?' asked Mrs Carelli. 'You can't just bring anything here, you know.'

'These things are my personal and private possessions, Mrs Carelli. So please, do your job and help me bring them inside.'

'I don't work for the Darklings. I work for the lad. 'Tis he that pays me, not you. So, no, I won't be helping you,' she told him, storming off inside.

An uncomfortable commotion followed. Stanley insisted that the house be split in two, and that he should keep the side where his bedroom was. The Darklings were

adamant that they should
be allowed access to the
whole house. But
Stanley stuck his neck
out and was backed
by Mrs Carelli and
Victor.

'May I remind
you, sir, that you
haven't proven
anything yet,' insisted
Stanley as he turned to
Mr Darkling. He found
it hard to stand up to
him, but he was making
himself do it. 'And as far
as I am concerned, we
have been more than
accommodating already.

So if you don't mind, that will be the agreement under which you are given the spare key to the house. Thank you for your cooperation.'

Stanley turned and walked away, a grin breaking across his face. Mr Darkling's eyes narrowed as he stared at Stanley, then he paced off noisily in the direction of *his* side of the house.

'Well done, lad. You stuck to your guns. You did right,' said Victor.

Stanley ran up the stairs and for the first time ever he locked his bedroom door.

Some time later he left, to seek solace with his friends out on the moor.

He left the house through the back door and escaped over the garden gate. But the crows spotted him, and once more he was forced to beat off their attack with flailing hands and arms.

When he reached the hills the cawing and crying of the birds petered away, and his mood lifted as he made out the faces of his friends. Big Bartley was chopping wood and wiping the sweat from his brow. The children were running around in circles and making the dogs bark. His good friend Phinn was feeding a hawk that sat perched on his gloved arm, and Stanley spent the next ten minutes watching it from close up as it feasted on the remains of a rabbit.

Greta's head popped out from inside her wagon, and she called him over. The younger children were fussing around Stanley, pulling at his shirt, eager for him to play, but she sent them away and Stanley could see that something was bothering her.

'Come inside, lad,' she beckoned. 'I have much to tell you.'

The roof of her small wagon was curved and shaped from old timber. Bits of heather hung from the ceiling and pots and pans, all beautifully painted, were scattered about. A table and seats took up the space at the far end and they sat down together.

'The glass ball has been hard at work, Stanley,' Greta began. 'I already know your predicament. It is some time since I set eyes upon the Darklings, but I am only too familiar with their bloodline. Now listen carefully.

'Many years ago, a keen businessman came to live on the Rock, and paid the locals to build a house for him. But to his great misfortune, he suffered an attack from the werewolf whilst returning home late one night. He survived, but he had been bitten, and fell under the werewolf's curse. And when he foolishly fathered a family, the blood of the beast ran through his veins and into those of his children.

'He was a good man, but eventually the curse overtook him and his animal antics became too much for his weakening body. In the end, it destroyed him. He left behind a widow and three boys. The strains of the beast showed in his offspring and eventually in their own children too. They were not werewolves, but their habits were almost dog-like. They ate raw meat and stalked the streets in a pack at night. They slept in the day and kept the whole village awake in the late hours with strange calls and howls.'

'And who was this man, the forefather to these people?' asked Stanley.

'His name was Brice Darkling,' she

Brice Darkling

announced. 'And what became known as the
Darkling Curse was familiar to the people
here for many years.'

'And the house that Brice Darkling built
for his family?' he questioned.

'Darkling Hall, Stanley.'

'I thought as much.'

'Edmund Darkling is a distant relative of
Brice. His family still bears the lupine traces.
He lived at the Hall until he was about your
age,' explained Greta. 'That is about all I
know, Stanley.'

They were interrupted by Bartley appearing
in the open carriage doorway. Bartley was a
huge man with a big heart, warm and friendly
but fierce and fearless when the need arose.
He held out a large hand to shake Stanley's.

'I don't know how you do
it, Stanley. Either trouble
follows you, or *you*
follow *it*. It seems
we have
another fight
on our hands,

although this time it looks like our boxing skills will be of no use.'

'There will be a way,' said Greta. 'There is always a way.'

Stanley's mood had dropped again by the time he returned to the Hall. Knowing that he must battle with the birds before he got through the door was bad enough, but now he had no idea what he might find inside. In the past, he had sought refuge in the house from all his troubles. But now his problems held him hostage inside his own walls.

Back inside, he straightened his ruffled hair and nursed the scratches on his hands made by the crows. The house was silent. Too silent. There were five more people living here now. Where were they, and what were they doing?

He walked down the dark corridor to his room, thinking troubled thoughts. And as he placed the key in the lock, a breathing noise sounded behind him. Somehow, he couldn't turn around. He froze, listening, and hoped that he had imagined it, but no – if anything, it was getting louder.

Stanley forced himself to turn and look.
At the far end of the corridor, the still and
brooding shape of a black dog stared back at
him. Where on earth had it come from? It
was huge, long and lank with its head held
low, its eyes fixed on him.

Carefully, he turned the key. And then
swiftly he tugged at the door and shot inside –
but he tripped on the rug and went sprawling
across the wooden floor. Four legs thundered
down the bare boards of the corridor and as
Stanley lay helpless he watched the hound
snake around the door. It raced at him and
stood snarling over him, saliva dripping from
its open jaws. Stanley shut his eyes tight. He
couldn't bear to watch it eat him alive.

'Steadman!' came a young voice. '*Steadman*.
Come here, boy.'

The dog turned and trotted innocently up

to Berkeley, who stood in the doorway.

'He only wants to play,' grinned Berkeley.

But Stanley was too shocked to say
anything. He simply got to his feet and
pushed his door shut, locking it on the inside
and wiping the sweat from his brow.

That night he barely slept. And over the
next few days he noticed a pattern emerging.

Through the hours of sunlight, the
Darklings were still and silent and confined
to their rooms. But as the night drew in they
would grow noisy, emerging from their sleep.

Wonderful
Daisy

It was the end of another day. As Stanley sat
on his bed, something caught his eye down on
the harbour: a flickering candlelight in Daisy's
bedroom window down at the lighthouse. To
anyone else it was just a light, but to Stanley
it meant that Daisy was contacting him.
Either she had information that would help,
or she needed him. And then she signalled

that she would arrive in the morning.

Stanley was outside, ready to beat off the crows, when she came the next day. He held a long garden rake and swished it around as they swooped down on the pathway.

Daisy ran through the falling black feathers and they raced inside. As they slammed the door shut, Mr and Mrs Darkling emerged into the hallway.

'It is not in the interests of the Rock to
be attacking the crow population, Stanley,'
began Mr Darkling. Steadman was lurking
behind him, making Daisy and Stanley
nervous. A low grumble emitted from the
dog's belly.

'You brought those birds here,' came a voice
from the kitchen. It was Mrs Carelli. She was
covered in flour and holding a spoon towards
him like a sword. 'It isn't the lad's fault he
has to protect himself and his visitors.
Come on, you two,' she said. 'We
have fresh bread in the oven.'

Later, the two friends went up to
Stanley's room. At the top of
the staircase, Steadman was
guarding the doors on the
Darkling side of the landing.

61

He got to his feet as they reached the top step and growled at them as they tiptoed by, petrified.

As they turned into Stanley's quarters, Olive and Berkeley appeared right behind them.

'Arghh!' cried Stanley. 'I wish you wouldn't do that!'

'Do you want to play with us?' they asked, speaking in unison.

'Er … no. I'm sorry, we're … busy. There is something important we have to do.'

They were saved by Mr Darkling. 'Children. Here, at once. Go to your rooms.'

In the safety of Stanley's room, behind a locked door, Daisy could finally work on her idea.

Across the surfaces of his bedroom furniture all kinds of papers were laid out. The deeds to the Hall, plans of the house, and a map of the

island. Daisy pored over the details. She asked
Stanley to take out the silver casket and
assemble the map pieces again.

'Mmmm. Exactly as I thought!' she said
jubilantly.

'What?' said Stanley. He was on pins,
waiting for her to explain.

She laid out the map of the island next
to the map from the
silver casket.

'Now do you
see it?' she
asked, grinning
wildly.

'No!' he
answered.
By now he
was getting
frustrated.

'The hole in the middle of the map, Stanley. It's not a hole at all. Don't you see? It's exactly the same shape as Crampton Rock.'

Stanley examined it more closely. She was right! What at first had appeared like a piece torn out of the middle of the map was in fact a carefully crafted hole the same shape as the island.

After all this time! Discovering the silver casket and finding the maps inside the candles had been a journey in itself, but to discover that what lay beyond the map was a long-lost secret of Crampton Rock sent an excited shiver down Stanley's spine. Where did the map lead to? What would it reveal? Could they keep it a secret? All these thoughts buzzed around inside his head.

They looked at the instructions again, starting from the top. Stanley mumbled out loud to himself, trying to make sense of what he read. But soon he realized his first problem.

'Daisy, we can't do this yet!'

'Why not?'

'Well, what if we find out where the map leads to and we discover something ... You know, something special and valuable. What would we do with it? My possessions are already in jeopardy. If I kept something here in this house I might end up losing it, along with everything else. I am already worried about losing the silver casket. Those Darkling children are proper little snoops, and they're already spending half their time spying on us. It might be simpler to deal with the Darklings before we explore the map.'

'You're right,' Daisy admitted. 'We need to bide our time until this crazy nonsense is over with.'

They put everything neatly away, in the
hope that soon they would be able to return
to the treasure hunt.

For the time being, Stanley was keen for
Daisy to join him in a small adventure. He
explained to her that he had grown concerned
at how quiet the Darklings were in the day.
As the sun shone down on the Rock, their
curtains stayed closed and their silence was
unnerving. But at night they became active
and strange noises echoed down the corridors.

'One night, Mrs Carelli left her bed to see
what was going on and she was so disturbed
by what she saw that she fled to her room
and locked the door,' he explained.

'And ... what was it?' quizzed Daisy.

'I don't know,' he admitted. 'She still won't
tell me! You must join me, Daisy,' begged
Stanley. 'I need to see what they are up to.

Will you come with me through the secret panels of Candlestick Hall to the Darkling side of the house?'

Daisy agreed. Stanley could see that she was not keen on his idea of spying on the Darklings. But neither was he. It was just something that had to be done.

Through all the excitement, a moment's distraction meant that Stanley had, unknowingly, let himself down. As he and Daisy left Stanley's room to head for the kitchen, the door remained unlocked.

Who killed poor Stanley?

The two heroes sat in the kitchen scullery, whispering their route through the house as they dined on Mrs Carelli's newly baked bread and devoured half a jug of fresh milk.

Within ten minutes they were crawling through the secret passageways that ran inside the walls of the building. Stanley had discovered some of these in the past but Daisy showed him that there were many more.

They made their way to the Darkling side still covered in crumbs and milk stains, giggling quietly as they sneaked along in the dark.

Daisy led the way. 'Quiet,' she whispered. 'We're close now.' It was likely that she knew the house better than anyone. Much of what she knew wasn't even on the original plans of the house. Stanley wondered what Brice Darkling had had in mind when he built these secret routes, all those years ago.

Soon they were alongside the Darkling quarters and Daisy peeked in through a wrought-iron grating. She could just make out the shape of Mr Darkling, lying asleep on the bed.

Stanley squashed up alongside Daisy and they watched Mr Darkling's upper body gently rise and fall. But it was not what

Stanley would have called sleep, not a curled-up, warm, enveloped snooze. No. Mr Darkling lay with his hands crossed across his chest in a cold, mournful doze that looked more like a short slice of death. He was still dressed in his sinister black outfit and looked like he should be staring out from an open coffin.

Daisy and Stanley peered around the room. Several glass tanks were scattered around, but they couldn't see what was in them. The room was clean and tidy but had a strange smell.

Steadman rose up from the floor, taking them by surprise. He rushed over to the vent, sniffing noisily and baring his teeth at them.

Mr Darkling woke with a start. 'What is it, old boy?' he asked and his face appeared up close, inspecting the grate.

Stanley and Daisy ducked their heads and hid in the darkness of the corridor.

If Mr Darkling had explored the house as
much as Stanley when he was a boy, he
would know the way in to the passage.

Mrs Darkling appeared. 'What is it,
Edmund?'

'I'm not sure, dear, but I think perhaps
we have visitors. Mice or rats maybe. Or
possibly something bigger!' He rubbed his
chin in thought.

Steadman was going crazy by this time,
snapping and snarling, and he woke
Annabelle and Olive in the next room.

By now Stanley and Daisy had shuffled along out of harm's way and were alongside the girls' room. They pressed their faces up to the next grating. The girls were sitting up in bed, clapping their hands together in sequence and reciting a strange verse that sent a chill from Stanley's head to his toes.

'Who killed poor Stanley? "I," said the Crow,
"With a shot from my bow, I killed poor Stanley."
Who caught his blood? "I," said the Fish,
"With my little dish, I caught his blood."
Who'll make the shroud ...'

'Girls, please. You make too much noise,' said Mrs Darkling, poking her head around the door. 'We are trying to sleep. You should be doing the same.'

Behind Stanley and Daisy, the familiar sound of panting was coming down the narrow passage. It was Steadman – Mr Darkling must have sent him in to investigate. They scrambled into a fast crawl as the noise of his breathing came closer. In desperation, Daisy pushed the grating out into the next room along and they burst through the hole, pulling the cover back over as they went. Fortunately, the room was empty, the covers pulled back on the bed.

It was Berkeley's room, but he was nowhere to be seen.

A strange smell filled the air. Sinister-looking wooden toys were spilled across the floor, and hand-marks and scribbles adorned the walls. What a mess!

What seemed like hundreds of little bottles, filled with liquids in all manner of

different colours, were stacked along the top
of a chest of drawers. Some of them bubbled
away and in one there was a cloudy
effervescence which looked like it might
burst the bottle open at any second.

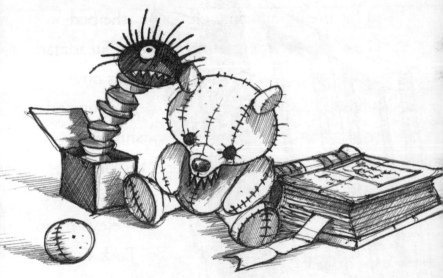

The sound of feet echoed from the
landing. Daisy dived under the bed and
Stanley instinctively jumped for cover under
the sheets, pulling them right over his head.

Only a fraction of a second later, Mr Darkling appeared around the door.

'At least someone has remained undisturbed,' he said as he glanced at the

lump in the bed. Steadman was now snarling and sniffing through the grating in Berkeley's room. 'Back to your bed, old boy,' instructed Mr Darkling as he closed the door and left.

'That was close,' said Daisy as her face peered out from under the bed. 'Let's get out of here before Berkeley returns.'

When they were sure that Steadman had cleared out of the secret passageway, they lifted the grating and climbed back in, taking a longer route to avoid going back the way they had come.

Stanley now knew that the Darklings slept during the day, and were most active by night.

And the verse that the girls had recited was ringing in his head.

They started descending a narrow staircase to the ground floor. Daisy remembered the little doorway that opened up into the chimney breast of the scullery, right back where they had started. Finally, Stanley peered out through the stony cold of the fireplace.

'Yep, it's clear,' he said, jumping down.

Covered in soot, they sat back down in their chairs and drank the last of their milk.

But all the while they had been searching on the Darkling side of the house, someone else had had the same idea. Someone who only Stanley and Daisy knew was missing from his bed. And as they scraped the breadcrumbs from their plates with sooty black fingers and drank the last drops from the milk jug, young Berkeley was creeping across the hallway back to his room, with his hands full.

The Old Candle Shop.

At breakfast, Victor was explaining his plans to Stanley and Mrs Carelli as they sat at the kitchen table.

'I cannot attend to the garden here,' he admitted. 'Every time I step outside the door the birds attack. It is the same for all of us. So I have decided to spend some time cleaning the candle shop. If they throw us out of here

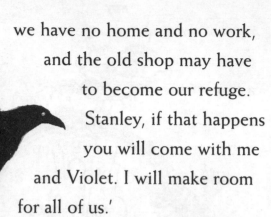

we have no home and no work,
and the old shop may have
to become our refuge.
Stanley, if that happens
you will come with me
and Violet. I will make room
for all of us.'

'You're very kind,' said Stanley.
'Not at all,' said
Victor. 'I owe you everything I
have. It was you who saved me
when I sat marooned out on
Scarecrow Point. Now I may
have to save you.'

'In that case, I shall come and help
you,' Stanley decided.

'Well in all my days I've
never heard anything like it,'
began Mrs Carelli. 'Here he is,

lord of the manor, sat in
his mansion and never lifting
a finger since the day he
arrived. But show him a bruised
and battered old candle shop and he's armed
with brooms and brushes and off like a shot.'

They all laughed out loud and for a
brief moment Stanley remembered the
time before the Darklings arrived and
how happy they'd been. Would it
ever be the same again?

They packed Victor's work
tools and put them into
a small cart. Mrs Carelli
made a large picnic bundle that
she placed in Stanley's arms
and then they set
off, beating off the
birds as they went.

Shortly they
were down in the
village, passing
through the square
and the hustle and
bustle of life, past
the old sweet shop
and the village
hall. They stopped
outside the old
candle shop on
the corner and
for the first time
in many years
the key
was turned
inside the
rusty lock.

Cobwebs tried desperately to hold the door shut, but soon they were inside. A damp smell hit them immediately, and Victor shoved the windows open.

He pottered around checking through boxes of candles and looking here and there for this and that while Stanley had a snoop around.

There was the shop at the front, and behind the counter was access through to the back rooms, and a back door leading out to the beehives. Beyond that was the moor.

One of the back rooms was larger than Stanley expected, a huge space where all the candles were made. There was a big vat like a bath in the middle of the floor, with worktop space around it. Candles hung on lengths of wick, suspended from ropes that ran from one end of the room to the other.

Upstairs, there were three smaller rooms: one with a tin bath and large jug in it, the others with beds, and everything caked in dust.

Soon they were hard at work, scrubbing the worktops and sweeping the floors. Victor stopped work for a minute to laugh at young Stanley working so hard – Mrs Carelli would have dropped to the floor to see it, he chuckled.

Someone rapped on one of the windows. It was Daisy, with a spare brush in her hand. She let herself in and they spent the day sprucing the whole place up. Dusting, washing, scrubbing.

And as they did, they knew Mrs Carelli was keeping her eye on the old Hall. They knew only too well that if they all left the house, even for just a short time, they would more than likely get locked out for good.

Daisy was busy washing the windows when she caught something familiar out of the corner of her eye. 'Stanley, look!'

He moved to the window. It was Berkeley, leaving a run-down old building across the way.

They were watching him with interest when Victor came to their side. 'I'm sorry, I neglected to tell you that.

The place opposite, it's the old Darkling place. Hopefully, they'll be returning there soon. Strangely enough, they used to be good customers here,' he continued. 'It is rumoured they spend most of their waking hours in the dark, and they've bought many candles here in the past.'

Stanley stared at the house opposite. It was ramshackle and shoddy, with decaying, rotten timbers and shutters fastened awkwardly across the windows. A crooked brick chimney capped off a rickety roof, and Stanley remembered that this was the place where he had seen the crows resting before the Darklings had come to Candlestick Hall.

Something is Missing

When Stanley and Victor returned to the house that evening, something had changed. The birds were perched on the far side of the roof and there was no swooping or clawing or diving down at their faces. Nothing.

Stanley was puzzled, until he caught sight of someone standing at the foot of the pathway. It was Phinn, holding his hawk on his arm.

Every few minutes he released her and she soared up into the air, circling over the house.

'Greta sent me,' he said, as they walked towards him. 'She said that soon you would return to the house and that I was to make sure the crows were kept at bay.'

Stanley watched the great hawk as she returned and landed on Phinn's outstretched arm. Though she was large and powerful, she was very graceful. She tilted her head and looked at them.

'She's beautiful,' said Stanley. He held out his hand gently and stroked the plumage on the underside of her belly.

'Careful, lad. She must like you. She'd normally take a chunk out o' something that came that close.'

Stanley knew how to win the confidence

of animals; it was something that came naturally to him. And he felt safe with the crows tucked away on the roof, even when he turned and caught Edmund Darkling peering out from behind a curtain. He enjoyed their brief moment of victory over the Darklings, and remembered what Greta had said to him. 'There is always a way.'

But as they stepped into the house, Stanley's mood sank. The Darkling children were playing in the hallway, and Mr Darkling was hanging a portrait on the wall. In the dim candlelight, Steadman pinned Stanley and Victor to the door.

'Mister Darkling, we can't be having the dog threatening us every time we walk in. It isn't fair,' said Victor. 'He should be confined to Darkling quarters.' The dog grumbled and stared at him like he understood every word.

'Get down, Steadman,' said Mrs Darkling, emerging swiftly and disappearing just as quickly, taking Steadman and dragging him awkwardly by his huge collar. She was such a small woman it was hard to imagine how she could muster up the strength.

'Mister Carelli, may I remind you that you are staff here,' said Mr Darkling. 'What's more, the hallway is a communal area, since it serves to allow access in and out of the building.

Steadman is showing signs of uneasiness in your presence. Perhaps he feels you are a threat to him.'

'And on another small matter,' continued Victor, ignoring him, 'you cannot make changes to the house whilst the ownership is in dispute. The documents clearly state this, so I'm afraid you'll have to take the picture of the little dog down from the wall.'

'It is not a little dog, Mister Carelli. It is a picture of my son Berkeley,' Mr Darkling said, red-faced.

'Oh. Begging your pardon, sir,' added Victor. 'I do apologize. I haven't got my glasses on.'

The residents dispersed with embarrassment, and a spell of silence reigned for a short time. But the dark had returned and Stanley knew the Darklings would be up to no good. He had come to realize that if there was a time to watch them, it was at night.

He sat up late in the scullery, tucked in front of the fire, reflecting on the day. When Victor had made his comment on Berkeley's portrait, Stanley had tried to hide his amusement, but he chuckled quietly to himself as he remembered it.

He drifted into sleep, only to be woken by a tapping from the darkness of the hallway. A voice accompanied it, too faint to be heard.

Stanley slowly raised himself up from his seat and edged over to look through the crack of the doorway. He couldn't see anything. He tiptoed into the hallway and followed the sound until it took him to the back of the staircase.

And there were Berkeley and Olive. Berkeley was holding a short stick and tapping on the pike's glass case.

'He's ugly, isn't he?' said Olive.

'Yes. And he moved, so he must be alive,' said Berkeley.

'He can't move. He's dead,' insisted Olive.

'He did. He moved. He moved his *eye*. I saw it,' claimed Berkeley, tapping harder and faster on the glass.

Stanley felt that he should intervene at this point, but as he stepped out into the moonlit hall the twins had set off chasing each other around the house, running across the floor on all fours.

Well, that explains the banging and clattering all night long, he thought.

'Stanley, I fear you may be losing your grip on the Candlestick estate.' Stanley swung around. It was the pike! They hadn't spoken for some time, not since the Darklings had first laid their gloomy shadow across his door.

'I should hate to become a part of the Darkling furniture,' continued the pike. 'I much prefer the company of your good self and your staff. Victor has made a wonderful job of my new home. What do you intend to do?'

'I don't know!' Stanley whispered. 'Not yet. But Greta says there is always a way.'

'Ah, the gypsy lady. A wise old owl, Stanley, I'm sure. Of course there is always a way. But will you find it?'

Just then, Stanley was thrown off course. 'Isn't it a little late for you, Stanley?' came a slow voice. Mr Darkling was standing in the doorway to the lounge, the moonlight picking out his face and his eyes glowing demon-like in the darkness.

'I fell asleep in the scullery. I'm going up now,' Stanley said, feeling as though he should explain himself. He hurried to climb the stairs.

'Oh and Stanley,' continued the voice behind him.

Stanley forced himself to stop and turn. 'Yes?'

'If I catch you or anyone else snooping around in my private quarters, I shall make sure my dog makes a fast meal out of your bony little frame. Do you understand me?'

'Of course,' Stanley said, trying to keep his voice steady. 'Why on earth would I want to do that?'

But when he reached his room his fright turned to anger, as he realized he had left the door unlocked the night before. Quickly he ran to his cupboard and pulled back the false panel. The space where the silver casket should have sat was empty.

'Oh no. No,' he whispered. He searched again, bringing the candle closer. Perhaps he had missed it. But no, it was gone.

'*Berkeley*,' he said to himself in a heavy tone. Berkeley was into everything. Climbing here, searching there, crawling under and over, weaving his way in and out of this and that, knocking things over,

breaking the vases that adorned the rooms.
He was like an oversized rat scuttling
around the place.

Stanley knew there was no point
confronting Berkeley. He would only
deny it. Instead, under the meagre
candlelight, he forgot all that had been
said and decided to work his way back
through the secret corridors.

But first he needed something from the
kitchen. He glided down the staircase and
slipped into the larder. Then it was back into
the scullery and up inside the chimney breast.

Even in his rush of anger, he did not really
like the idea of entering the Darkling domain
at the dead of night. He had only escaped
discovery the last time by the skin of his
teeth. This time he was alone and the way
ahead was pitch black.

As he grew near the Darkling quarters
he could hear music, the deep and
sombre sound of something slow
and funereal. As Stanley
peered through the grating
to Mr Darkling's room,
he could see that it
was empty.

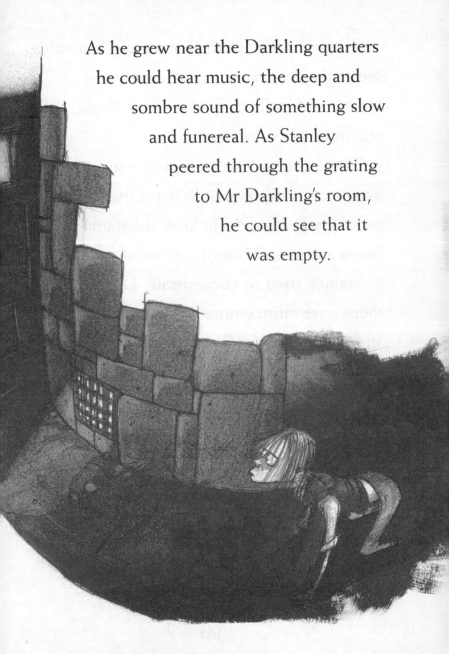

A light burned in the corner and he could see something moving in the glass tanks, hissing and rattling. Snakes! Real, living, moving snakes.

The darkness up ahead of him suddenly grew more frightening. What if the snakes could move around, slinking about under the floors and in and out of the walls?

Stanley tried to concentrate. Up ahead there were more empty rooms, first the girls' and then Berkeley's. But there was no sign of the children. Where were they? Quietly, he levered open the grating to Berkeley's room and stole inside, taking care with the candle in his hand.

He eased open every drawer. Nothing. The casket could be in many places – it was small and compact – but he had a feeling Berkeley had not spent much time in his room. Nothing seemed to have been moved since his last visit.

Stanley searched harder, listening to the music continuing somewhere nearby. But still, nothing.

Pausing a moment, Stanley realized that the music was coming from the rounded tower that perched on the gable end of the house. He was eager to see what was going on, and he knew he could peer through the ceiling of the tower if he got into the loft. He poked his head around the doorway of Berkeley's room into the dim light of the corridor.

Sensing that no one was there, he made his way across the passageway on finely tuned tiptoes. He pulled gently at a section of wainscoting, disclosing a cobwebbed doorway that probably only he knew about.

But something had touched his neck. Something cold and damp. Little by little, Stanley turned around. It was Steadman, pinning him to the wall with the point of his nose.

The whites of the dog's eyes were fluorescent in the dark. Stanley sensed the heaviness of a bark welling up inside Steadman's throat. But before it happened, Stanley slid his hand into his pocket and handed the dog a chunk of red meat.

That was all it took. Steadman's head jolted as he threw the meat back into his mouth and ground his teeth into the tasty morsel. Then he slung it greedily down his throat and looked excitedly at Stanley. Another piece came. And then another.

The music continued as Stanley got ready to make his final move. He dangled a final

piece at Steadman, patted the dog's head as
he caught it and then disappeared behind the
panel. The last piece of meat was still in his
pocket. He knew he might need it on the
way back.

Steadman stood mesmerized. Where had
his newfound friend gone? The pleasant-
looking one with the meat who he had
thought was his enemy, but suddenly realized
was not so bad after all.

Meanwhile, Stanley had made it into the
circular lofted area over the tower. The
music was closer and louder now, slow and
sombre. He tried to see down through the
boards, but the gaps were tiny and he only
caught glimpses here and there. Finally, he
found a spot where he could see half of
the room.

It was Mrs Darkling making music at this late hour. She sat with a large double bass, her beady little eyes closed, moving her head gracefully as she played.

Mr Darkling was there also, standing up and holding something in both hands.

It was a large glass bell jar. Stanley had to narrow his eyes to concentrate on what was inside it. It appeared to be a black snake, contained in a liquid, and Stanley was certain it was some mutated form as it seemed to bear two heads.

Mr Darkling held up the jar and closed his eyes. He whispered something through the glass and Stanley was sure that as he did so the snake shifted slightly in its prison.

He knew that the Darkling children were there also, although he could only see their feet as they sat together on a long cushioned seat.

Mr Darkling opened the top of the glass jar. It was only Stanley's excellent knowledge of the animal kingdom that let him recognize what he was seeing. The sleek black form wound its way upwards out of the liquid and, as Mr Darkling watched with a contented expression, it slithered away under the floorboards.

Stanley had seen enough to know that what was heading towards his side of the house. It was a black Crow Snake!

To add to his horror, the girls began to repeat the verse again.

'Who killed poor Stanley? "I," said the Crow,
"With a shot from my bow, I killed poor Stanley."
Who caught his blood? "I," said the Fish,

"With my little dish, I caught his blood."

Who'll make the shroud? "I," said the Beetle,

"With my thread and needle, I'll make the shroud."

Who'll dig the grave? "I," said the Owl,

"With my pick and shovel, I'll dig the grave."

And what of the Hall, empty and bare? Who will take care?

"We," said the children. "Along with our kin, we shall step in.

We will take care."'

The music stopped and the verse ended. Stanley sat in shock. He realized that the Darkling plan was far more sinister than he could possibly have imagined.

He wheeled his way quietly back through

the loft and descended the stairs. When he opened the door in the panelling, Steadman was waiting for him. The dog whined pathetically and lifted a paw to Stanley until he handed him the last morsel of meat.

Stanley stroked Steadman's head and scratched his chin. He had made a friend. But somewhere beneath the floorboards, the snake lay waiting for him.

Tell-tale
Signs

On Stanley's return to his room he frantically covered over every conceivable gap in the floor. Curled up in a tight ball on his bed, he looked up the Crow Snake in his book.

> **Crow Snake (Karasu-hebi)**
> Can grow to two metres. Will curl up with its tail vibrating in a similar manner to the rattlesnake and strike aggressively, with its mouth wide open.

Stanley couldn't possibly sleep. He had seen the snake's movement, sleek and swift. He decided it would probably have reached his room even before he did. Perhaps he should rip up the floorboards and find it.

But what if he'd only *thought* he'd seen it? Maybe it wasn't coming to get him at all, and the girls had only made up their chant in jest.

He didn't know what to think. Eventually, his body couldn't hold out any longer and he drifted into a heavy sleep. Soon he was dreaming.

As he dreamed, the dreadful verse rang in his head. He was walking out upon the moor among the birds and long grass, but he could hear the girls' high voices singing, and the deep, listless tones of the double bass. He wandered near the lake and stood in the water as the cold wash lapped around his bare feet.

He heard the rush of the reeds in the wind and as he stood, the wind in his face, the bulrushes began to rattle.

Stanley woke with a start. He knew what that rattle meant! He looked down and saw the coiled-up snake in front of him, poised to attack. His mind began to work at frantic speed. How could he move more quickly than the time it would take for the snake to strike?

The situation unfolded as if in slow motion. The snake's dreadful double head lunged upward at him, two open mouths revealing the sharp, poisoned pincers concealed within. Stanley ducked backwards, banging his head on the headboard, clutching desperately at his bedclothes. The black snake got caught up in them, and thrashed wildly as Stanley wound the sheets round and round. Finally, he was sure that it was securely wrapped up inside them, and taking the broom from the corner of his room, he beat it and beat it until he was breathless and convinced that what lay inside was dead.

With the lifeless snake thrown to one side, Stanley fell flat upon his mattress in exhaustion and didn't stir again until morning.

When he finally awoke the next day, he cautiously unravelled the motionless snake from the sheets and placed it in a box in his cupboard.

There was every chance that this strange evidence might come in useful.

Stanley sat on the edge of his bed, thinking about the events of the day before. Berkeley jumped into the front of his mind. Where was the silver casket? Stanley tracked back to the previous day down at the old candle shop and recalled that they had seen Berkeley down at the old Darkling place.

It made perfect sense. If Berkeley had wanted to keep the silver casket from Stanley, it would be a good idea to take it back somewhere Stanley didn't even have access to.

Despite his long night, Stanley was up and about before Mrs Carelli had even stirred. Only Victor was around, digging through more paperwork before he set off for the candle shop. 'Just doing a little more research,

lad,' he said, lifting his head for a brief
moment and looking over his half-moon
glasses.

Stanley was the first to see that there was
post waiting on the mat. Two identical-
looking envelopes, one for Mr Darkling and
one for Master Buggles. Stanley left the first
and opened the second. It was from the
village hall: a hearing would be held at the
Crampton courtrooms in a week's time, to
decipher ownership of the Hall.

He showed it to Victor, and decided he
would explain what had happened in the
night. By the time Stanley had finished his
tale, Victor was shocked. He jumped to his
feet. 'Where is this ... snake?' he asked, in his
most concerned voice. 'Do you still have it?'

'It's still in my room,' said Stanley.

'Bring it down, lad, and leave it with me.

115

The more evidence we have, the better.'

Stanley brought down the box containing the snake and promised that he would be back later. He sprinted down the path before the crows had awoken to his presence.

Down in the village the world was stirring. The fishermen had already left for the open sea. A smell of fresh bread drifted from the bakery, and doorways and windows were opening here and there.

Daisy trotted up behind Stanley. 'You're up early!' she said, full of early-morning cheer. She was clutching a crusty loaf.

'So are you!' he answered.

'No, Stanley, I'm always up at this time. It's just that you're not around to see me! What's wrong?' she asked, sensing an uneasiness in his manner.

116

'The casket, Daisy. It's missing,' he
announced. 'I know it was Berkeley who took
it, and he was here yesterday, right? It's in the
Darkling place, it must be. What do we do?'

Daisy accompanied
Stanley to the old candle
shop and they hung
around outside it,
eyeing over the
rotted wooden
shack that was the
old Darkling
place. Daisy's good
knowledge of Crampton Rock was about to
come into play again. It was something she'd
found out long ago about the houses in the
village: most had quick-access flaps or
doorways built in to ensure a swift escape
from *things of the night*, should the need arise.

117

It was likely that the Darkling house also had one, and if so it would be the best way in.

When Stanley and Daisy were sure that no one was looking, they crossed over to the old place to have a snoop around. Sure enough, behind the rickety wooden steps at the rear of the building there was a small square hatch with rusted hinges. Inside, a shaft of light gave way to the sudden appearance of Stanley Buggles' inquisitive head, breaking a long spell of empty darkness.

Inside, the house was bare and unappealing. A stale smell filled the air and Stanley felt the urge to pull back the shutters, but Daisy stopped him. She knew they must conceal their occupation of the house. Dust particles swam around in the shafts of light that sneaked through the rotten wooded panels.

There was nothing here. Nothing but

empty rooms, creaking floorboards and damp walls, both upstairs and down. Old keys and scribbled notes lay on the windowsills. A small bowl of nails rested in the hearth, and a dusty black coat hung over one of the doors.

'I don't think it's here, Stanley,' said Daisy. She peered out through a gap in the down-stairs shutters.

Mr Darkling was approaching the front door, with Annabelle at his side.

'Quick, Stanley!'

Their eyes scanned the room hastily, searching for hiding places. Time was running out. The door creaked as Mr Darkling stepped in and Annabelle followed.

'Arghhh ... nothing!' cried Mr Darkling.

'What is it, Father?' begged Annabelle.

'Still no post,' he muttered. 'I await contact from my brother, important papers that I will need. But it is late. Perhaps tomorrow.'

He walked into the front room and sniffed the air, his eyes shifting suspiciously from side to side.

'What is it *now*, Father?' asked Annabelle.

'Either that Buggles boy has been here, or his scent is jammed up my nose. But somehow I don't think he'll be bothering us any more,' he quipped. Finally they turned and left, locking the door behind them.

Stanley and Daisy climbed down from inside the chimney breast, covered in soot.

'That was almost as close as last time,' laughed Stanley.

'I can't handle all this,' gasped Daisy. She was still holding the loaf of bread in her hand, but now it was black and looked like it had been burned.

They left through the hatch, covering their tracks as they went. Daisy breathed in the fresh air, relieved to be out. But it was only a temporary relief.

'Hang on, Daisy. We need to go back in,' announced Stanley.

'W-what for?'

'There was a telltale sign, and I almost missed it!' he began. When he'd stood on the ledge inside the chimney breast, he'd been staring into the little pot with the nails in … and only half thinking.

'Explain, please!' said Daisy.

'I *bet* they're floorboard pins,' Stanley said. He pushed his way back inside the hatch, and Daisy followed him reluctantly. 'All we have to do is go back and find the creaking boards.'

121

They separated and trod carefully through the house, Daisy checking the staircase first.

'Here,' cried Stanley. 'Down here.' Daisy thundered down the shaky staircase to see Stanley trying to get his fingers into a gap between some boards, looking around for something to help him. He picked up one of the nails from the bowl and forced it down the crack. Levering the edge of the board ever so slightly with his foot on the long nail, he slid his fingertips underneath and pulled upwards.

A dust cloud choked their throats. When it had settled, they looked inside.

There underneath the boards, thrown carelessly on its side, was the familiar shape of the lost casket. A beam of a smile crossed Stanley's face as he pulled it out and checked it over. Everything was still inside it, untouched.

No doubt Berkeley had placed the casket there so that he might take a good look when he was able to return.

'No chance of that!' grinned Stanley.

As he and Daisy made their way back to the hatch, they heard someone climbing the steps to the front door. It was the postman; he had only just reached the bottom of the village. And now here he was, pushing a letter addressed to Edmund Darkling through the door.

Without pausing for thought, Stanley slipped it inside the casket, and they left.

Stanley didn't think it a good idea to wander through the village with the silver casket, as Berkeley had done, so they stole across the road to the candle shop. By now Victor was there, and they told him everything.

Vital Evidence

For now, they decided to hide the silver casket in the shop. Victor was not entirely happy about this, fearing the old days of unsavoury pirates darkening his door, but Stanley insisted that, for the moment, the place was without suspicion.

Stanley was pleased with his find, but he was angry with Berkeley. Deep down he wanted to punch him on the nose, but Berkeley was nowhere near his size. And anyhow, he hoped his revenge would be to take the house back and send Berkeley home, and that almost made Stanley feel sorry for him.

Under the hooded safety of the candle shop, Stanley and Daisy sat in the back room with the silver casket proudly on the table-top. When Stanley had double-checked and triple-checked that all the pieces of the map were there, he studied the letter he'd taken from the house.

Daisy expertly steamed open the envelope over a pan of boiling water, to make it look like it had not been tampered with. Then she handed the letter to Stanley, who unfolded it to reveal a short handwritten note.

My dear Edmund,

I trust you have made your move and laid claim to Candlestick Hall. I will send this to your house in case you are delayed, but by now you should be settled into the Darkling estate.

Shortly I will be with you, and once again the Darklings will rise. We set sail in a month's time. Both myself and my dear wife Marianne are eager to join you back in the family seat where we belong.

I hope our plans to be rid of the boy have been fully realized. If he remains alive he will only uncover our false claim on the estate. As promised, I enclose the forged deeds which I have had scribed by an expert in these matters. Take great care with these. Such devious strategies do not come cheaply. They have been made to look old, and so the parchment is torn and folded.

We will arrive in due course.

Meanwhile, I remain your affectionate brother,

Ludwig

Daisy read the letter in shock. But Stanley was grinning from ear to ear.

'Stanley!' exclaimed Daisy. 'They plan to be rid of you for good, and in the meantime they've forged the deeds to your house – and you're sitting there smiling! Don't you understand, they're going to kill you!'

'Daisy, wait! Please, don't panic. Their plan has already failed. Last night I watched in secret as Mister Darkling laid a deadly plot. He charmed the dead body of a harmless mutated two-headed snake into a lethal living creature, then he sent it under the boards towards my room. I captured it, and struck it until it was dead. Right now, Mister Darkling thinks I am lying lifeless upon my bed. But the truth is that I am alive, and I have been handed the evidence that will seal the fate of the Darklings.'

Victor's head appeared around the door. 'What is all the excitement about?'

'Take a look, Victor,' smiled Stanley.

Victor read the letter carefully. 'Where did you get hold of this, Stanley?' he muttered. 'We must present it in the court when the time comes.'

They placed it carefully in the silver casket, then found a hiding place for the casket beneath the floor of the old candle shop, until it was needed again.

'In the meantime, the rest of our evidence is coming together nicely, Stanley,' Victor informed him. 'I spoke to the court on my way here about bringing Doctor Peebles in as a witness.'

'Doctor Peebles! But what has Doctor Peebles got to do with any of this?' quizzed Stanley.

'Don't worry, lad,' said Victor, smiling. 'It will all become clear at the trial. You don't need to concern yourself with the details, not yet. I did some investigating of my own after you told me of the snake incident.' He gave Stanley a look that said he knew what he was doing.

Stanley and Daisy headed out of the back entrance to make their way across the moor and visit the gypsies.

A strong smell of roasting meat drifted in their direction as they approached the camp, and they joined the group sitting around the fire. Warm drinks and cooked meat were handed among the families, as Romany tales of long ago began to circulate. The dogs hung around greedily and stared at the meat with expectant faces. Stanley picked at the bones and fed them small chunks.

Phinn piped up. He wanted to tell Stanley and Daisy the story of when the gypsies had arrived on the island, all those years ago. The two friends pricked up their ears and settled into comfortable positions.

'There is no place like the Rock. It is the centre of the earth. Some say that once, the devil came here on horseback. That the hooves of his black mare were so fiery hot that they seared their shape into the very stones that lay across the land. Now, the grass grows so long and the wind blows so hard at that lofty point that no one would ever venture there and find out if it was true.

'When we travellers first came here, Stanley, there was nothing. Nothing but cold hard wind and the bleak moor. None of us was even born then: it was our fathers that came here and settled. They were free and happy and survived off the land. But their peace was short-lived.

'The curse of the wolf began to plague us. At first, we noticed howls at night and that the sheep were slowly disappearing. And

then, before long, the dogs also. Of the ones that remained, all were three-legged, a sure sign of sinister struggles in the night.

'And then our first real loss. Wheelbarrow Wallace. Strong as an ox and our bravest warrior, taken one night whilst making his way home from the harbour. The first of many. They reckon the beast was badly wounded in the struggle that night.'

'Like my brother, Ned,' said Bartley. 'He was taken one night, as he slept outside. Lucky for the wolf he wasn't awake,' he chirped. 'He would have torn it apart.'

'And my Uncle Bill,' said Phinn, jumping in. 'Went one night to take out the beast with a shotgun. And all we found next day was the still-loaded weapon and a pile of bones with every bit of meat licked clean off!'

Daisy stared uneasily at the chump in her hand. Stanley secretly passed what was left of his to the dogs.

'We came back here when we discovered you had destroyed the beast,' continued Phinn. 'We live in the hope that it will never return.'

'There is no prospect of that,' said Greta. 'Here on the Rock and in other such strange places, darkness delivers the curse of the wolf. Not the fullness of the moon, nor any other such nonsense. It is sown in the soil of the land. The curse lives and breathes in the earth.'

'Rubbish!' a woman cried out. 'There are no wolves here, not any more. They can't appear out o' nowhere.'

'Remember what you say, sister,' said Greta, with fire in her eyes. 'Because tomorrow I will remind you of your words, and one day they may come back to haunt you.'

Stanley and Daisy huddled nearer each other, spooked by the talk of the wolf's return. The younger children had heard too much and they were being put to bed as Daisy urged Stanley that they should make their way back.

They decided to go down through the village and head up through the square.

After all the wolf talk, they had no desire
to cross the bleak moor in the oncoming
darkness.

It was much later when Stanley arrived back
at the house, having accompanied Daisy to
the lighthouse. The crows descended as
usual, only this time there seemed to be many
more. Four or five flapped around his ankles,
pecking and cawing, and another ten or
maybe twelve were beating their wings about
his head and scratching at his face. He fell to
the floor, kicking helplessly at them until
Victor came out and beat them away.

He picked himself up and they hurried
inside. The whole house had stirred at the
commotion, and everyone was assembled in
the hallway.

The Darklings were dumbfounded to see

Stanley. They had not glimpsed him all day, and Mr Darkling had been hoping his sinister midnight plot had worked.

Stanley decided to say nothing about the snake. He would hang on to the story along with his evidence, and pretend he knew nothing in the meantime.

Mr Darkling eyed him suspiciously, but he knew he could say nothing. His plan had failed and though he longed to know why and how, he knew he could not question the circumstances.

He had still not received the mail he awaited from his brother, and his claim to the house would look thin and weak without the forged deeds.

It had not been a good day for the Darkling cause.

Berkeley was glaring at Stanley too. He

had been back down to the Darkling house earlier, only to discover that the silver casket was missing from beneath the floor. He had no proof, but he was sure that Stanley had claimed it back.

Berkeley knew he could not ask for it when he had stolen it in the first place.

'You think you're clever, Stanley,' he whined. 'Well, maybe I'm just that bit more clever than you, Bark!' Stanley quipped, feeling pleased with himself.

'What did you call me?'

'Bark. It's your new name. Seeing as how Victor thinks you are a little dog,' Stanley grinned.

Berkeley deadened his eyes at Stanley, and beckoned his trusty hound. 'Kill, Steadman. Kill.'

Steadman went pounding over to Stanley, smelled the meat from the gypsy camp on his hands and licked him lovingly until an annoyed Berkeley pulled him away.

'How did you do that, Stanley?'

'Do what?' Stanley asked innocently.

'Make him *like* you. How did you make him *like* you like that?'

'As you say, Bark, I'm clever! Woof woof,' Stanley shouted as Berkeley turned to leave the room.

Berkeley edged back inside the door and

stared hard at Stanley. And then he growled menacingly at him, baring his short pointed teeth and turning up his little snub nose. He held his hands out like claws.

Stanley would have been frightened, had he not been so amused. 'Run along now, Bark. There's a good boy.'

'Stanley, you make me so *cross*. You think you're big and clever and you never, ever, EVER play with me,' said Berkeley, and he ran out of the room in tears.

And Stanley felt a trickle of guilt run through him.

All that this sinister little boy *really* wanted, more than anything else, was someone to be his friend!

Silence in Court

The courtrooms stood in one corner of the village, overlooking the square. They were a series of long rooms at the top of one of the buildings, and gave a good view out to sea.

A whole group of people were milling around, waiting to be allowed in. Stanley's nerves drummed around inside him and he felt a fluttering feeling in his stomach.

Miss Spoonbill was
present, along with two
older gentlemen, one
thin and one fat.

A Mr Barker and a Mr Rook. Their faces looked old and grumbly. Perhaps they wouldn't like the idea of the young boy with his own mansion, thought Stanley.

There were court officials everywhere, and Stanley recognized them as people from the village, dressed in black robes and strange pieces of headwear. The court made it clear that they were not allowed to greet Stanley but one man, a local fisherman, gave him a knowing wink and he felt spurred on by it.

Finally, they filed through the door and sat in high-backed chairs around a table that ran the length of the room. At one end was a cubicle with people who Stanley knew must be the jury, the people who would make the final decision. He knew there were faces from the village, but he tried not to look.

Then in walked a small, frail man,
who appeared to be almost lost
under his robes. Everyone
was invited to be
upstanding for Judge
Angus Bumble and
when he had sat down
they all followed.

The Darklings
bunched up opposite
Stanley, the children
sitting still and silent. Berkeley had been given
strict orders to keep himself under control.
He, Annabelle and Olive fixed their stares on
Stanley, never seeming to blink or move.

Miss Spoonbill opened the session with
some long speech that Stanley couldn't get a
grip on. Instead he scribbled a picture of a
small dog and held it up discreetly, but so

that Berkeley could see it across the table.

Maybe it was the nervousness of the court-room or perhaps something else, but for the first time, Stanley saw Berkeley break into a chuckle. The chuckle became a laugh and then the laugh became a clout on the back of Berkeley's head from Mrs Darkling.

'Silence in court while the judge blows his nose,' came a loud voice. Judge Angus Bumble fumbled in his robes, took out a handkerchief resembling a tablecloth, and began to clear his snout noisily.

It was too much for Berkeley. His fit of giggles had begun and the nose-blowing incident only made him worse.

Stanley was stronger. He knew a fit of giggles would not go his way in court and he held on to his resolve, concentrating his thoughts on what lay ahead.

'Let us begin,' said the judge when he had
folded his hanky away neatly.

Firstly Mr Darkling
spoke. He told of his
family history on the
Rock. How he had
spent his childhood at
the Darkling estate, and
how it had been taken
from his parents by
Admiral Swift, a cunning
and merciless buccaneer. And that the paper-
work to prove his claim was on its way.

'You make a feeble case, Mister Darkling,'
suggested Mr Rook. 'Without any form of
evidence, you accuse Admiral Swift of piracy
and of the theft of your home. If you have
paperwork that proves your case, it should be
present in court.'

'But the Hall is still filled with our things. My family name is written in stone upon its very walls,' claimed Mr Darkling, gritting his teeth and staring at Stanley.

'I'm afraid,' continued Mr Rook, 'that only serves to confirm it was built for Brice Darkling. It gives you no entitlement to the estate.'

'But the boy,' Mr Darkling growled. 'He is not fit to run such a place. He has brought nothing but trouble here. Only recently, the whole place was swarming with pirates.'

'Nonsense!' burst out Mrs Carelli. 'We've always lived in fear of piracy out here on the Rock, long before the boy came here. 'Tis ridiculous to claim he is responsible.'

It was time for Victor to bring forward the evidence on behalf of Stanley. He was armed with piles of papers and a small box with a flimsy lid.

'When you're ready,' asked Mr Barker. He had a low gentle voice and a kind smile, and Stanley shook off the instinct that told him he was old and miserable.

Victor joined Stanley. 'Here is the proof of purchase regarding the sale of Darkling Hall to Admiral Swift by Edmund Darkling's father. Here is the proof of Stanley's family connection to Admiral Swift, bearing in mind he left no will and that the laws of Crampton Rock entitle the youngest family member to the estate. And, of course, here are the deeds belonging to Stanley Buggles for the presently named Candlestick Hall estate.'

'Thank you, Mister Carelli. Thank you. I think that is enough to be going on with. Mister Darkling, is there anything you wish to respond with at this point?'

'I wish to postpone these proceedings,'

cried out Mr Darkling. 'I am still awaiting
vital evidence that will prove my claim.'

'I think we have the evidence that Mister
Darkling speaks of!' suggested Victor. All eyes
fell on him.

'Continue,' said Judge Bumble.

Victor read out the letter from Mr
Darkling's brother Ludwig that explained the
plans to forge the deeds to the Hall and,
much worse, to be rid of young Stanley. The
whole courtroom gasped in surprise.

'Silence in court, please,' Mr Barker called.

'Murderers!' It was Bartley shouting and
shaking his fists.

Mr Barker got to his feet. 'And how did
you come by this information, Mister
Carelli?'

'Well ... we took it, sir. We took it from
the house,' struggled Victor.

'You took it from *which* house?' continued the investigation.

'From … the Darkling house, sir!' Victor admitted.

Gasps went up. The court was stirring with 'ooh's and 'aar's as Stanley jumped to his feet.

'It was me, sir. I took it from the Darkling place. I shouldn't have … but … but I was desperate to get hold of the truth, sir!'

'Sit down, please, Master Buggles,' asked Mr Barker. He waited a moment and when Stanley had composed himself, he continued.

'Do you mean to tell me that in collecting your evidence for this court, you broke into a house in the village and stole mail belonging to someone other than yourself?'

'Yes … sir. Although I didn't really see it that way, it's just that—'

But he was stopped in his tracks.

'Mister Barker, am I right in thinking that Master Buggles is explaining that he obtained his evidence by illegal means?' questioned Mr Bumble.

'Yes, sir, I think that is the general idea of what he is explaining.'

'Then you must remind him that this court does not accept any form of evidence acquired in such a manner.'

'Of course, sir. Yes I will.' Mr Barker repeated this to the court and instructed the jury that they should not take this evidence into account.

'Could we have the next piece of evidence please?' asked Mr Rook.

Unshaken by the events so far, Victor took

the lid from the box and lifted the dead body of the snake on to the table. There were more gasps as Stanley explained what had happened.

'Will you please be quiet. I will have no choice but to adjourn this court if we cannot view the evidence under civilized circumstances ... Thank you,' said Judge Bumble, as the noise dissolved into a whispering hush.

'Mister Darkling, perhaps you wish to comment on the presence of a snake in the boy's room, and your plot to be rid of him?' suggested Mr Rook.

Mr Darkling stared hard at Mr Rook. 'I know nothing of this,' he claimed. 'It is irrelevant. The house is full of such curiosities.'

'And you claimed earlier that all of those deadly objects are yours?' smiled Mr Rook.

Again, Mr Darkling was lost for an answer. A whisper passed between several court officials.

'Could we call a Doctor Peebles, please?' asked Mr Barker. A stringy-framed man lolloped into the room and made his way to the front. He was carrying a large case and seemed to be blissfully unaware of what was going on or why he was there at all.

'Doctor Peebles,' began Mr Barker, 'could you tell the court what you do here on the island.'

'Well, yes of course. I'm the village doctor here, sir,' he said, peering over his half-moon glasses with his back hunched over as if it couldn't bear the weight of his head.

'Not much call for anything serious here on the Rock, I wouldn't have thought,' suggested Mr Barker.

'Well, no, but the fishermen often come to me with strange bites and stings after a day out on the ocean. There are thousands of unknown toxins in those waters, sir! It's quite common for me to deal with those.'

'And how do you go about dealing with that? Where do you get your remedies?' Mr Barker questioned further.

'Well, I have a supplier of antidotes,' the doctor explained.

'And what are these antidotes made up of?' pressed Mr Barker.

'We use snake venoms, sir,' Dr Peebles explained. A whispered, knowing rumble ran around the jury box.

'Quiet, please. Do continue, doctor. Do tell

us who your snake expert is,' asked Mr Barker.

'Well, it's Mister Darkling, of course. He is a snake breeder and an excellent toxicologist.'

The excited whisper grew louder and again the court was told to hush.

'And what of the snake we asked you to examine? What did you make of that?' continued Mr Barker.

'It was a black Crow Snake, sir. Not known to be poisonous, but it had been mutated, do you understand? It had been altered to carry a poison. Typical of Mister Darkling's work, sir, he is a genius I must say, I—'

'Yes, thank you Doctor Peebles. That will be all,' finished Mr Barker. The jury were on their feet. The spectators' cries rang out again.

'Murderer! Send him down!'

'Silence in court.' Out came the large handkerchief again and the judge cleared his nostrils before he began to speak.

'We are veering away from the case here.
If you feel we have clearly established a false
claim upon the Hall, you must reflect this
in your judgment. If you feel the case is
unclear, you must be sure to push aside your
emotions and face the facts. Make your
decision wisely. The incident with the snake
must not influence your decision over the
ownership of the Hall. A separate hearing is
likely to follow regarding attempted murder.

And do not forget
that any evidence
gathered under
dubious circumstances
is deemed irrelevant.

'Let us adjourn so
that you may make your
decision.'

156

A tense period of waiting followed.
Stanley shuffled in his seat, his palms
sweating. Berkeley tried to make him laugh,
but it was not the right moment for that.

Finally, the court assembled itself back into
position.

'Jury, are you ready to give your decision?'
asked Mr Rook.

A small round man with spectacles stood
for the jury. 'We are,' he announced.

'And what have you decided?' continued
Mr Rook.

The man read from a short statement on a
scrap of paper.

'We, the jury, have together recognized
that the evidence produced by Buggles and
Carelli cannot be recognized and is therefore
not part of this case.'

Stanley's heart sank into his stomach.

'Master Buggles is new to the island and as the court is aware, all newcomers have to be officially accepted by the community, should they wish to stay. It is not in the interests of the Rock that such criminal activity occurs and as a jury we are naturally swayed by it.'

Stanley sank further into his chair. A feeling of great shame washed over him and the realization that he had put everything at risk by entering the Darkling home hit him hard.

'But there is nothing to suggest that the Darkling family have any legal claim on the estate presently known as Candlestick Hall,' continued the man. 'Their attachment is purely emotional and therefore by residing within its grounds they are trespassing on the estate belonging to Stanley Buggles.'

Gasps of relief came from Stanley's side of the room.

'Silence in court,' came a familiar voice. 'Judge Bumble will now speak.'

All eyes were fixed on the frail man stooped in his seat at the head of the room.

'Edmund Darkling, you have seven days to gather your belongings and return with your family to your home in the village. This court recognizes Stanley Buggles' claim to the Candlestick estate.

'I understand, Master Buggles, that in a moment of desperation you did something that was foolish. May I remind you that in future you should wait until invited before stepping through the door of any property.

'Regarding the seriousness of Edmund Darkling's attempt on Stanley Buggles' life, further inquiries shall be made.

'This court is now ended.'

Judge Bumble stepped down from his perch and left the room.

A fevered excitement surrounded Stanley and Victor. And at the same time a black cloud hung over the Darklings as they gathered themselves together.

The two sides collided in the doorway as they left the courtroom. Berkeley ran out into the street, trying to make Stanley chase him. He had no real understanding of the situation. Mrs Darkling rushed past, tears running down her face, but Mr Darkling stopped and turned to Stanley.

'You will live to regret this, young Buggles. You haven't seen the last of me.'

12

Back to Candlestick

As they walked through the village, Stanley
caught sight of Daisy waiting for them.
Mrs Carelli had asked her to look after the
Hall during the hearing. She hadn't trusted
the Darklings not to arrange some sinister
goings-on while they were all out.

Daisy was dancing around from toe to toe
in her anxiety. But when Stanley was close

enough for her to see his face she knew
immediately that the news was good.

As they neared the Hall, the crows were
making a most terrible din, much louder than
they had ever made before. Swooping down,

they seemed to be making a last-ditch
attempt to be rid of Stanley and the Carellis.
A huge black swarm of beating wings flocked
around them, stabbing at their faces with
sharp beaks and clawing feet. Loose feathers
filled the air. Stanley, Victor and Mrs Carelli
batted them off, with injured hands flailing.

'Edmund, stop it. It serves no purpose.
Stop them, now,' came Mrs Darkling's voice
from the foot of the pathway.

Mr Darkling let out a strange howling cry.
Every single bird stopped and swooped back
on to the roof. The victims nursed their
injured faces as they struggled in through the
front door.

An awkward period followed at the Hall. The
Darklings were of course extremely unhappy
at the jury's decision, and they knew that

sooner or later Mr Darkling would face the court again. But in the same breath, Stanley rejoiced at the good news and his side of the house erupted with joy.

'Daisy, now we can spend our time working out what the map shows,' said Stanley excitedly. They were sitting on the bare floor of Stanley's room with drinks and cakes, poring over the instructions.

'I was looking over it whilst you were in court,' Daisy said, 'and I think there's something odd about the map.'

Daisy was right. The way seemed to wind in twisting turning steps through what they were sure was the village square.

'To go from one end of the village to the other, you would go in a straight line. There's no need to wind this way and that,' said Stanley.

'Yes, but hang on,' started Daisy, 'this map is old. Very old. It goes back to when this place was different, when great hills and giant rocks stood here, before the houses. The way along here at one time might have been through a winding pass surrounded by huge trees.'

'Daisy, how do you do it?' laughed Stanley. 'I would never have thought of that in a million years.'

Right then, a shuffling knocking sound came from outside the bedroom door.

Stanley opened it quickly to find the Darkling children peering in through the keyhole.

'What do you want?' he asked.

'Berkeley has made you something, Stanley,' Annabelle and Olive said at the same time.

'What … what is it?' he asked, eyeing it suspiciously.

'Something to say thank you for letting us stay,' they all replied.

Berkeley handed a smeared and hand-marked painting of something four-legged to Stanley.

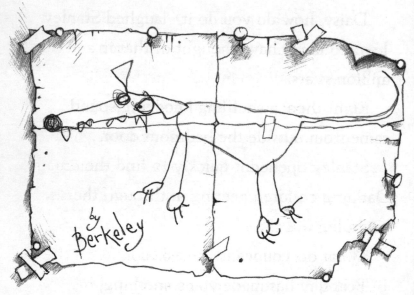

'Oh … er that's … nice,' said Stanley awkwardly. 'What is it?'

'It's Steadman,' said Berkeley as if Stanley should have known immediately.

'Of course it is,' Stanley answered. 'It's fantastic! Thank you so much.'

'We know you like him really, so we thought you might want something to remember him by.'

The familiar *click click click* of Steadman's feet sounded across the wooden floor and he appeared beside them, wagging his tail.

Stanley patted his head and stroked the underside of his chin. Secretly, Stanley had developed a growing admiration of Steadman and now Steadman loved him back. He was just a big old softy.

Daisy exchanged surprised looks with the Darkling children. Berkeley shrugged his shoulders and chuckled.

'Come on,' Stanley said, and Steadman

trotted down the staircase after him. Stanley sneaked quickly into the larder and pinched a handful of meat, feeding it to Steadman before the Darklings realized what he was up to.

But Mrs Darkling had spotted that they were all together. 'Come on!' she shrieked. 'Back in here at once. Steadman, here boy!'

'I'll see you soon, Stanley Boogles,' said Berkeley.

'*Buggles*. It's Buggles,' corrected Stanley.

'BOOGLES!' insisted Berkeley and he chuckled, revealing his sharp grin.

'All right, BARK. I'll see you later,' Stanley smiled.

'Woof woof,' said Berkeley.

Steadman raised a final paw to Stanley before leaving and Mrs Darkling pierced him with her black eyes before slamming the door.

'Well, well, Stanley. Things seem to have turned out for the best.' It was the pike, managing to make himself heard from his place on the wall.

'You even managed to get the hound to eat out of your hand. Most impressive, Stanley. Darkness is lifting from the house already. I couldn't have stood that dreadful boy a moment longer.'

'Yes, I know,' said Stanley. 'It has been quite a strain. But I almost feel sorry for them now I've seen the house that they must go back to. It is a dreadful place, run-down and ramshackle. I hope I never have to go there again.'

'Oh, you'll change your mind about that, I'm sure,' said the pike. 'The old Darkling place is not as insignificant as you might have thought.'

'What do you mean by that?' asked Stanley, but the pike had decided, as he often did, that he was not going to say any more.

The · the
Final Twist

The next morning, the Darklings were
preparing to leave. The first thing that
Stanley noticed was the crows flocking from
the roof and heading down into the village,
where he presumed they had returned to the
old place. The beating and flapping of a
thousand wings, the cawing and crowing of
every beak made a terrible noise.

But it was as if a dark cloud had lifted from over the house and the sun was allowed to shine on them again.

The Darklings gathered their things and began to load them back into the old cart.

'I don't want to watch them leaving,' Stanley said to Victor and Mrs Carelli. 'It feels bad-mannered, as if I'm gloating. Come on,' he said, turning to Daisy and adding in a whisper. 'Let's go and investigate. Can we go over to the candle shop, Victor?'

'Of course, lad,' Victor said, and handed him the door key from a piece of string about his neck. 'I'll be bobbing along myself soon.'

And as the Darkling family moved their meagre belongings out of the house, Stanley and Daisy headed into the village, the map concealed in Daisy's pocket.

They knew that when they next returned

to Candlestick Hall it would be back to normal and they would be at peace.

It only took Stanley and Daisy around an hour to crack it. They sat in the candle shop again, the map out on the table, and studied it hard until they agreed that they had understood it in the same way.

They left the shop and traced their way back to the starting point, which they were sure was at the harbour, and measured their way carefully along the route described on the map.

It meandered here and there, twisting and turning, and they imagined passing through the winding route of trees that had once stood there.

Then it took them away from the village and they headed back towards the moor,

past the village hall. Stanley pushed ahead,
climbing the rocks.

'Wait!' said Daisy. 'We turn right here,
under the old watchtower.'

'But that takes us back into the village,'
Stanley argued. 'We'll be back at the candle
shop.'

Daisy shrugged her shoulders. 'Check it,' she said. So he did.

'You're right, Daisy. You're definitely right,' he agreed and they veered back into the village.

'We're almost there, Stanley. There's not far to go.'

Stanley and Daisy looked around them. The cobbled streets were alive with people.

'This could prove to be very difficult,' said Stanley, scratching his head.

'Come on,' said Daisy. 'We have to find where it leads to!'

Stanley paced the way that Daisy read out to him, measuring the distances with his bandy-legged stride. Daisy walked behind him, her head down, not looking at what lay up ahead. 'Stanley, do you realize that we are about to uncover what must be something very ancient and very, very valuable?' muttered

Daisy. 'This map is so old it is almost falling apart in my hands. You have no idea what this could mean. Fame and fortune. Untold riches,' she laughed. 'Just ten more paces north of where you are now, Stanley, and that's it. X marks the spot, as they say.'

'Oh ... oh dear,' said Stanley in a troubled tone. 'This is it, Daisy. This is where our precious treasure lies!'

'What?' asked Daisy. 'What is it?' But as she looked up, she knew. Stanley was standing directly in front of the old Darkling place. The shutters banged in the wind and the flock of crows stared down at them, cawing and flapping their shrouds.

'It's *here*,' Stanley said, looking right at her. 'It's right here, where this building stands.'

And just then the sound of rolling cart-wheels came up behind them. The Darklings, returning with all their belongings. They pulled up to the front of their old home. Edmund Darkling unlocked its worn and weathered entrance and watched his family step inside. He gave Stanley Buggles a cold, hard glance and then he closed his door on Crampton Rock.

Scribbles from the

Something Wickedly Weird

sketchbook

Bert

Chris Mould

Chris Mould went to art school at the age of sixteen. During this time, he did various jobs, from delivering papers to washing-up and cooking in a kitchen. He has won the Nottingham Children's Book Award and been commended for the Sheffield. He loves his work and likes to write and draw the kind of books that he would have liked to have on his shelf as a boy. He is married with two children and lives in Yorkshire.

Crampton Rock seems the perfect place to spend a long summer holiday. But there's always something to go and spoil it all, isn't there?

Why are all the **dogs three-legged?** Is there really a **werewolf** on the loose? And what do the *pirates* want with Stanley Buggles...?

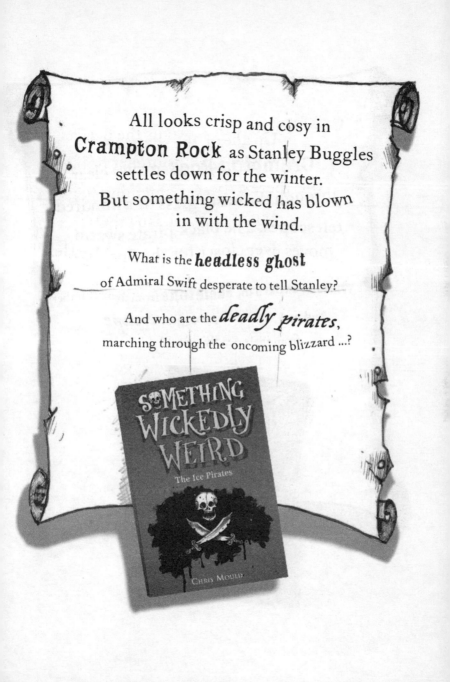

All looks crisp and cosy in **Crampton Rock** as Stanley Buggles settles down for the winter. But something wicked has blown in with the wind.

What is the **headless ghost** of Admiral Swift desperate to tell Stanley?

And who are the *deadly pirates*, marching through the oncoming blizzard ...?

SOMETHING WICKEDLY WEIRD
The Ice Pirates

CHRIS MOULD

Up ahead, the shape of **Crampton Rock** grows clear through the misty glass of a hundred telescopes. The black pirate swarm moves ever closer for the final battle.

What has awoken the **skeletons** from their slumber? And how can Stanley Buggles *escape* from their deadly grip ...?

SOMETHING WICKEDLY WEIRD

The Buccaneer's Bones

CHRIS MOULD

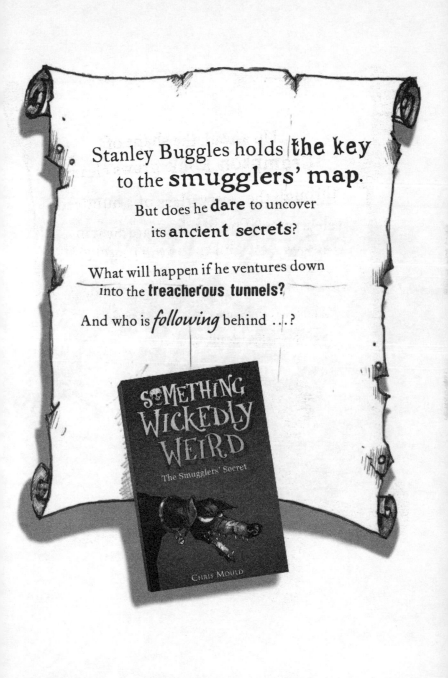

Stanley Buggles holds **the key** to the **smugglers' map**. But does he **dare** to uncover its **ancient secrets**?

What will happen if he ventures down into the **treacherous tunnels?**

And who is *following* behind ...?

SOMETHING WICKEDLY WEIRD
The Smugglers' Secret

CHRIS MOULD

Are you prepared to be scared?

This book contains ten of the most terrifying tales, adapted, written and superbly illustrated by award-winner

Chris Mould

Five are original ghost stories, and five are retellings of classic tales, from *The Legend of Sleepy Hollow* by Washington Irving to *The Tell-Tale Heart* by Edgar Allen Poe.

Open this book at your own peril ...